FISHING: TIPS & TECHNIQUES™

BOWFISHING

JASON PORTERFIELD

rosen publishing's rosen central

New York

Published in 2014 by The Rosen Publishing Group, Inc.
29 East 21st Street, New York, NY 10010

First Edition

Library of Congress Cataloging-in-Publication Data

Porterfield, Jason.
Bowfishing/Jason Porterfield.—1st ed.—New York: Rosen, © 2014
p. cm.—(Fishing : tips and techniques)
Includes bibliographical references and index.
ISBN: 978-1-4488-9489-5 (Library Binding)
ISBN: 978-1-4488-9500-7 (Paperback)
ISBN: 978-1-4488-9501-4 (6-pack)
1. Bowfishing. 2. Fishing—Juvenile literature. I. Title.
SH459 .P67 2014
799.1'4

Manufactured in the United States of America

CPSIA Compliance Information: Batch #S13YA: For further information, contact Rosen Publishing, New York, New York, at 1-800-237-9932.

CONTENTS

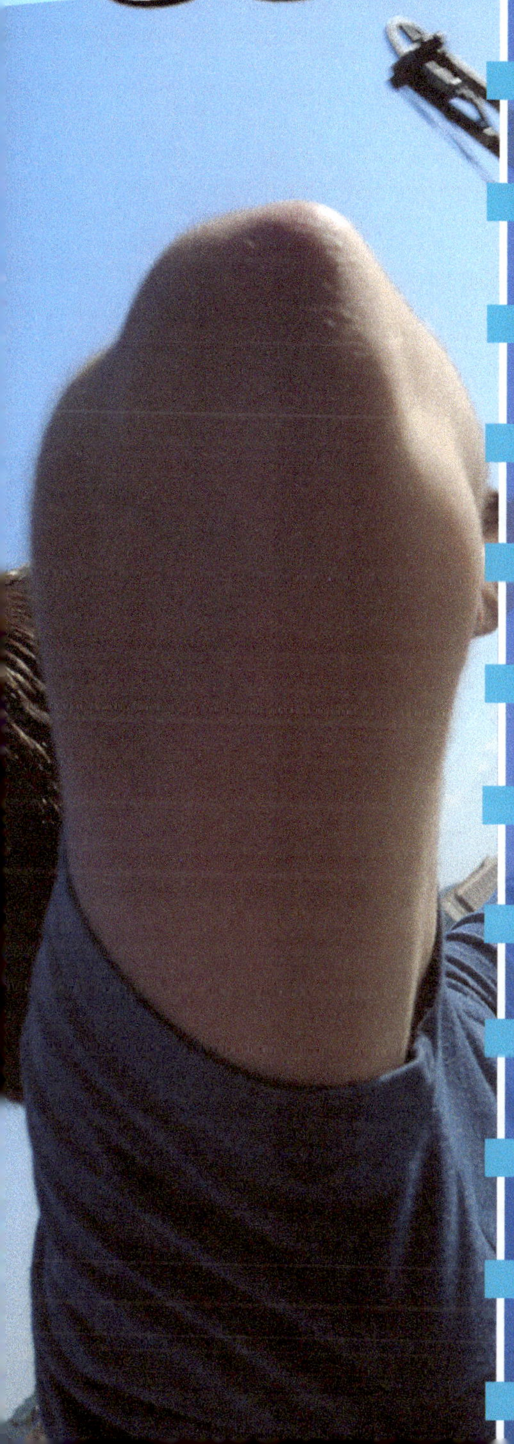

INTRODUCTION

A boat rests on the surface of the water, its engine silent. Lights shine onto the water as an archer stands in the front of the boat with his bow raised. He notices movement below the water's surface and spots a carp. Within seconds, he releases his bowstring, and an arrow speeds toward the carp accompanied by a trail of fishing line. The arrow strikes home, and the man uses a reel attached to his bow to bring the carp into his boat.

The man in the boat is a bowfisher, one of a small but rapidly growing segment of sport fishers who use their archery skills to target fish. Bowfishing has been practiced in many cultures around the world but only started catching on in the United States within the last thirty years. At first, bowfishers had to make or improvise their own equipment. Today, manufacturers market specialty bows, reels, and arrows to bowfishing enthusiasts.

Bowfishers are a very specialized group within the long and rich tradition of fishing. Many bowfishers are also archery hunters or bow enthusiasts. Often, they are introduced to the sport by a friend or a relative who bowfishes. Some of them go bowfishing when bowhunting season ends, or they may

Using a bow and arrow is a unique but incredibly exciting way to catch fish. It requires lots of practice and skill to excel, but the payoff is huge. This bowfisher has just nabbed a garfish.

warm up for bowhunting by going on bowfishing trips. Others may not have any interest in game hunting. They prefer being out on the water and looking for fish to hunting game on land.

Those who fish with a bow and arrow share a love of the outdoors and an interest in wildlife. They enjoy the thrill of catching fish. Many of them specialize in bowfishing and don't often use other, more typical fishing techniques requiring a rod and reel. They may devote a great deal of their spare time to fishing, target practice, and improving or upgrading their equipment.

Bowfishers still make up a relatively small segment of the fishing population, but the sport is catching on with archers and fishers. Like other fishing enthusiasts, bowfishers pass on their knowledge of the sport to first-timers, newcomers, and future generations. Tournaments and all-night fishing excursions give bowfishers ample opportunity to build traditions for years to come.

CHAPTER 1

Bowfishing Safety and Sportsmanship

Archers and fishing enthusiasts of all kinds often form tightly knit communities. Bowfishing is no exception. Bowfishers may get together to practice their archery skills, talk about equipment, and scout out new locations to ply their skills. Some go on fishing outings together. It is not unusual for more than one bowfisher to be in a boat for a night of fishing or for more than one boat to be fishing at the same location. Bowfishers are often enthusiastic about their sport and are willing to help others learn the ropes.

Bowfishing Tournaments

Many bowfishers are brought together by tournaments. These tournaments are held in many states where bowfishing is legal. They combine the unique challenges of bowfishing with the universal excitement of a competition. Tournaments can be small

A bowfisher aims an arrow while standing on an airboat in southern Louisiana.

events without a prize payout that attract mostly local bowfishers. Larger tournaments might bring in bowfishers from other areas or even from out of state and may last for a few days. In "ironman" tournaments, competing bowfishers may be shooting for twenty-four hours straight. They are often sponsored by bowfishing clubs, sporting goods companies, and other businesses. These tournaments may include equipment vendors and representatives from bowfishing clubs or other organizations that promote wilderness activities. Prizes might be awarded to the winners.

Tournament formats can vary widely. They may be held on rivers or on lakes. Competitions commonly follow a "numbers" or a "Big 20" format. In a numbers competition, the person who catches the greatest number of the targeted fish within a set time wins. In the Big 20 format, the winner is the person who catches the twenty heaviest fish by the end of the tournament. Big 10 or Big 5 tournaments, in which the number of fish weighed is much smaller, are also common.

Some bowfishers are very serious about tournaments. They may be focused on winning or on establishing a personal best in terms of the number or size of fish caught. Former tournament winners may be looking to defend their titles, and novice bowfishers may be eager to prove themselves among others. Many other bowfishers, however, go to tournaments simply to have fun. They socialize with others who share their passion and enthusiasm for the sport and check out the boats and bows that other bowfishers use. Bowfishers who are new to the sport can make new friends and pick up valuable advice at these events.

Hazards on Land and Water

Bowfishing is an exciting and challenging sport. It can also be dangerous if safety precautions aren't followed. Any activity that takes people out on the water can be treacherous. An added element of danger for bowfishers is that they often fish at night. It may be nearly impossible for rescuers to find a bowfisher who falls into the water at night. Bowfishers should know how to swim and avoid fishing alone in case something goes wrong.

Bowfishers should wear lifejackets at all times when they are out on the water. In fact, they may be required to do so by state law. It is also a good idea to keep an extra lifejacket or flotation device and a safety

Because accidents happen, all bowfishers, no matter how experienced, should wear a life jacket to ensure water safety.

line in the boat. These can be thrown out to someone who has fallen into the water. A first aid kit should also be kept on board in case of an accident.

Some bowfishers wade in the water or bowfish from the shore. Waders can be more vulnerable to strong currents or sudden drop-offs below the water's surface. Walking over slick rocks can cause a wading bowfisher to slip. He or she may either go underwater or be injured by falling on rocks or even his or her arrows. Wading into rushing water can be extremely dangerous, as the fast-moving current can knock a bowfisher off of his or her feet. The unlucky bowfisher might be swept downstream or smashed against rocks. Wading bowfishers also might be sucked underwater by strong currents.

For these reasons, wading bowfishers should wear lifejackets and be careful about where they fish. Wearing no-slip wading boots can help bowfishers maintain their footing on slick rocks or against strong currents. Wading bowfishers should always fish with a partner who can help or seek emergency assistance if anything goes wrong. It is particularly important that wading bowfishers know the area where they are bowfishing. They should have knowledge of how fast the water typically moves, what slick rocks might be in the area, and where they can wade without stepping into a hole.

Bowfishers who fish from the bank should also know their territory. Banks can crumble underfoot, sending the bowfisher down into the water. People who are just starting out in the sport should confine themselves to areas where the water is no more than 2 or 3 feet (0.6 or 0.9 meter) deep at the bank. In some areas, there may even be quicksand to navigate.

Wildlife can also be a hazard in remote areas. Alligators and poisonous snakes, as well as bears, wildcats, and large mammals, such as moose or bighorn sheep, can pose a threat. Bowfishers who fish from the shore should be aware of what potentially dangerous animals are

Arrows should always be pointed at targets only, such as these flying Asian carp in the Illinois River. Always be aware of people around you, on a boat, wading in the water, or standing on the shore. Never aim an arrow at anyone or anything other than the desired fish.

common in the areas where they fish and when these animals are active. They can find out where dangerous animals have been sighted by talking to other bowfishers, game wardens, and hunters. They should familiarize themselves with the correct steps to take to avoid encounters with dangerous wildlife.

Bow Safety

Archery can be a dangerous sport. Arrows are designed to pierce a target. An arrow can kill or seriously injure a person if he or she is hit by one. All bowfishers, whether they are in a boat, wading, or on the shore, should be aware of where their arrows are pointing at all times. Never draw back a bowstring with an arrow nocked unless the arrow is pointed at an intended target. Arrows that are not nocked should be pointed in a safe direction as a way to avoid accidentally stabbing or cutting oneself or others.

Bowfishers should be aware at all times of anyone else nearby on land or in the water. When shooting a bow, archers should make sure that they have a clear line of sight on their target and that no one is within the line of fire. In most cases, bowfishers are shooting their arrows into the water, so someone wandering into the line of fire is unlikely.

Fishing with a bow carries two major risks for the bowfisher. Sometimes, arrows can strike a rock or some other underwater object and be deflected. Deflected arrows could fly off in another direction and hit someone else, though the flight of these arrows would be restricted by the line attached to them. Bowfishers also face the possibility of a snapback. This is when the line connecting the arrow to the

Cabled Arrows and Safety Slides

Snapbacks can cause serious injuries or even death. The danger of snapbacks can be reduced by using a cabled arrow specially made for bowfishing or a device called a safety slide. A cabled arrow is an arrow that features a piece of wire or strong line running from the arrowhead to the end of the arrow. A two-way fishing swivel is attached to the line in such a way that it can move the length of the line. When the arrow is released, the swivel is near the arrowhead and keeps the line to the front of the arrow. It doesn't slide to the back of the line until the arrow strikes its target.

Safety slides work in the same way. These inexpensive rings are made to slide along the shaft of the arrow. The fishing line is tied to the ring, which is set near the arrowhead before firing. When the arrow strikes, the ring slides back along the shaft until it hits a stopper attached to the arrow near the end of the shaft.

reel becomes tangled with the bowstring and the arrow flies back at the bowfisher. Snapbacks are most commonly caused by tying the line to the back of the arrow. When the arrow is released, the trailing line can form a loop, which can tie itself to the bowstring, the arrow rest, or even to a wristwatch, causing the arrow to fly back.

Fishing Etiquette

Fishing enthusiasts have a responsibility to keep sites as clean as possible, so that fish and other aquatic wildlife can thrive and other fishers can continue using the spot. Most fishers follow common-sense standards for fishing behavior, whether on public or private land. If bowfishing on private land, fishers should always make sure that they have permission to do so from the landowner. Bowfishers on public land should make sure that bowfishing is allowed in the area that they are using.

Whether on public or private land, bowfishers should be careful to never leave any arrows, lines, or other equipment behind in the water. Lines can snare fish, birds, and other animals, while arrows can cut and stab them. Avoid leaving litter behind or dumping fuel or other chemicals in the water. Doing so can cause environmental damage and spoil a site. It is also against the law and punishable by a steep fine and even jail time. Also, never leave behind fish that have been killed or any of their remains, such as innards. Doing so ruins the site for other fishers and is illegal in many places. It can also attract dangerous wildlife, like bears.

Responsible bowfishers work with local and state game officials to protect sites. Many bowfishers pick up litter left by others and report any environmental damage that they notice. Some bowfishers consider it bad form to shoot fish while others are nearby. They also avoid using loud generators and bright lights when bowfishing near homes at night. Being courteous and considerate of others and respecting bowfishers

Respect and protect the land you are fishing on by keeping it clean and safe. Litter and pollution will harm the fish populations, water quality, and surrounding environment you rely upon as a bowfisher.

and nonbowfishers alike is the best way to make sure that areas remain open to bowfishing.

Getting a License

Getting a license for bowfishing is usually a simple process. Most states require only that bowfishers get a sport fishing license. Some states on the East or West Coast may require a special license or a stamp for saltwater bowfishing and for bowfishing in coastal areas. Most states do not require an archery permit for bowfishing.

Bowfishing is usually permitted in any waters where other types of fishing are allowed. People bowfish in rivers, creeks, lakes, swamps, and even drainage ditches and canals. Bowfishing is allowed in some coastal areas, as well. Bowfishers should check with local and state game officials to find out which waters are open for fishing. Bowfishing seasons vary from state to state but typically begin in late spring and run through late fall. Many states open their seasons in May, after fish have spawned earlier in the spring.

Fish that are commonly caught by bowfishers include carp, gar, perch, suckers, catfish, and eels. In saltwater areas, sharks and stingrays are usually targeted. Some states even allow bowfishers to catch alligators. Each state regulates what fish can be caught, so it is necessary to check local laws before starting.

States set a daily catch limit for bowfishers. Limits may vary greatly. The limit may be high for one species, but quite low for another. States also may limit bowfishers to targeting fish of only a certain size. In some cases, a permitted species can be caught only in specific places and not in other nearby areas.

CHAPTER 2

Bowfishing Equipment

Getting started with bowfishing can be as easy as buying a license, attaching a reel to a bow, and getting some bowfishing arrows. As they become more deeply involved and experienced in the sport, bowfishers may seek out more specialized equipment specific to bowfishing, such as bowfishing rigs or bow-and-arrow accessories.

Choosing a Bow

Any kind of bow can be used for bowfishing. A bowfisher should choose a type of bow that he or she is comfortable using on or in the water. Many people who are just starting out in the sport put a bowfishing reel on a bow that they already own. This could be an old or a spare bow, or even a bow used for archery hunting. Others buy bows that are specifically marketed for bowfishing. These can cost hundreds of dollars.

All bows are made of flexible materials that are designed to bend back as the string

These carp were no match for this bow and the sharpshooting bowfisher who nocked, aimed, and shot the arrows.

is drawn. When the string is released, the potential energy created by the bending bow is converted into the velocity of the arrow. Most bowfishers today use compound bows, which were first developed in the United States in 1966 and patented in 1969.

Compound bows use a system of cables and pulleys called cams that turn when the string is drawn back. The string is harder to pull back at the beginning of the archer's draw than with other types of bows, but the cams make it easier to hold the string back before firing. The design makes it possible for the bow to store energy more efficiently than more traditional bow designs.

Traditional Bows

Historically, bowfishers used bows made from wood or bone. These bows had strings made from animal sinew or from natural fibers. Bows varied in size based on cultural preferences. Bowfishing was widespread among indigenous groups throughout South America, the Pacific Islands, and Asia.

For centuries, the recurve and straight bows were the most commonly used by hunters in the United States. A straight bow, such as a long bow, has a slightly curved shape. This type of bow is easy to draw back at first, but the drawing weight and tension increase as the string is pulled further back. A recurve bow curves out and away from the archer so that its tips are facing toward the target. This shape allows the bow to store more energy than a straight bow can.

There are still hunters who prefer other types of bows, such as recurve and straight bows, and these bows are sometimes used for bowfishing. Some archery enthusiasts may use one type of bow in one setting, and another type in another setting.

Crossbows, which are very powerful bows that are drawn using a crank device, are permitted in most states for use by people with disabilities. These bows can also be fitted with a bowfishing reel. Bowfishers who want to use a crossbow will probably have to seek and obtain a special permit.

Caring for Bows

Bows are easy to care for and ordinarily need little in the way of maintenance. Most modern bows are made of fiberglass or composite materials that hold up well with use. However, there are additional steps that a bowfisher can take to keep a bow working at an optimum level for years to come.

Avoid shooting a bow without an arrow. The weight of an arrow slows the bowstring down and reduces the amount of shock caused when the bowstring is released. Shooting without an arrow puts extra stress on bows and can damage them.

Regular cleaning, drying, and maintenance of a bow, especially after each use, will extend the life and improve the functioning of the equipment.

Try to keep bows dry. This might be impossible to do when bowfishing, but always be sure to wipe wet bows dry with a soft cloth before putting them away. Storing bows wet can damage the string and cause rust to accumulate on metal parts. Many archers oil metal parts to prevent rust. It is always a good idea to wax the bowstring to keep it from separating. It may be necessary to rewax the string if it gets wet. Store the bow in a cool, dry place. High heat can damage a bow. Be sure to unstring the bow when it is not in use. Because there is so much tension in the string, keeping it on when not in use can damage the bow by putting stress on its limbs.

Choosing Sights and Rests

Modern bows can be equipped with sights that allow archers to hone in on their target. Bows used for bowfishing can also be fitted with sights, though they differ from those found on hunting bows.

Not all bowfishers use sights. Some bowfishers find that sights are too cumbersome to work with at night. Many simply sight along the arrow shaft when aiming at fish. However, there are different sights available for archers who prefer a more precise means of honing in on their target.

Sights usually consist of pins set a certain distance apart within a circle. The target is sighted between these pins. Some bow sights have telescopic lenses to help archers zero in on game animals. Aiming grids are often used by beginning bowfishers and those who have trouble adjusting for refracting light.

Several manufacturers sell laser sights that are specifically designed to target fish at night. Some laser sights are built into bowfishing arrow tips and are designed to shine a laser beam directly on the targeted fish when the bowstring is drawn all the way back. The laser beam bends in the water to reach the targeted fish and shows the precise point of impact. These laser points can be expensive but are designed to be used over and over again.

Like sights, arrow rests are accessories that are installed on bows in order to help the archer shoot more accurately. The rests are designed to hold the arrow straight and level. Rests come in many different shapes and sizes. They are generally inexpensive, at least when compared to sights. Some rests are marketed directly to bowfishers, but regular archery rests can work just as well. Bowfishing arrows are typically heavier than regular hunting arrows, so choose a rest that can handle a little extra weight. Bowfishers who want to use a rest may want to try several kinds before settling on a favorite.

Reels, Arrows, and Other Equipment

There are three types of fishing reels that are typically used for bowfishing: hand-wrap, spincast, and retriever reels. Hand-wrap reels are made up of a circular spool around which fishing line is wrapped by hand and then held fast in a slot. When the arrow is released, the line is freed from the line holder slot and spools off after the arrow. The bowfisher then pulls the arrow back in by using a hand-over-hand motion. Hand-wrap reels are easy to care for and set up, but it can be hard to use one to reel in an arrowed fish that is still alive and struggling.

Spincast reels feature spools that are enclosed by a nose cone to protect the spool mechanism. When the arrow is shot and the line plays out, the bowfisher can reel it back in using a crank on the side of the reel.

Retriever reels are made specifically for bowfishing. When the arrow is shot, the fishing line spools out of a small bottle mounted on the back of the reel. To retrieve it, the bowfisher pulls a trigger and turns the side crank.

Hand-wrap and spincast reels can be inexpensive, and some bowfishers even make their own hand-wrap reels. Retriever reels, however, are

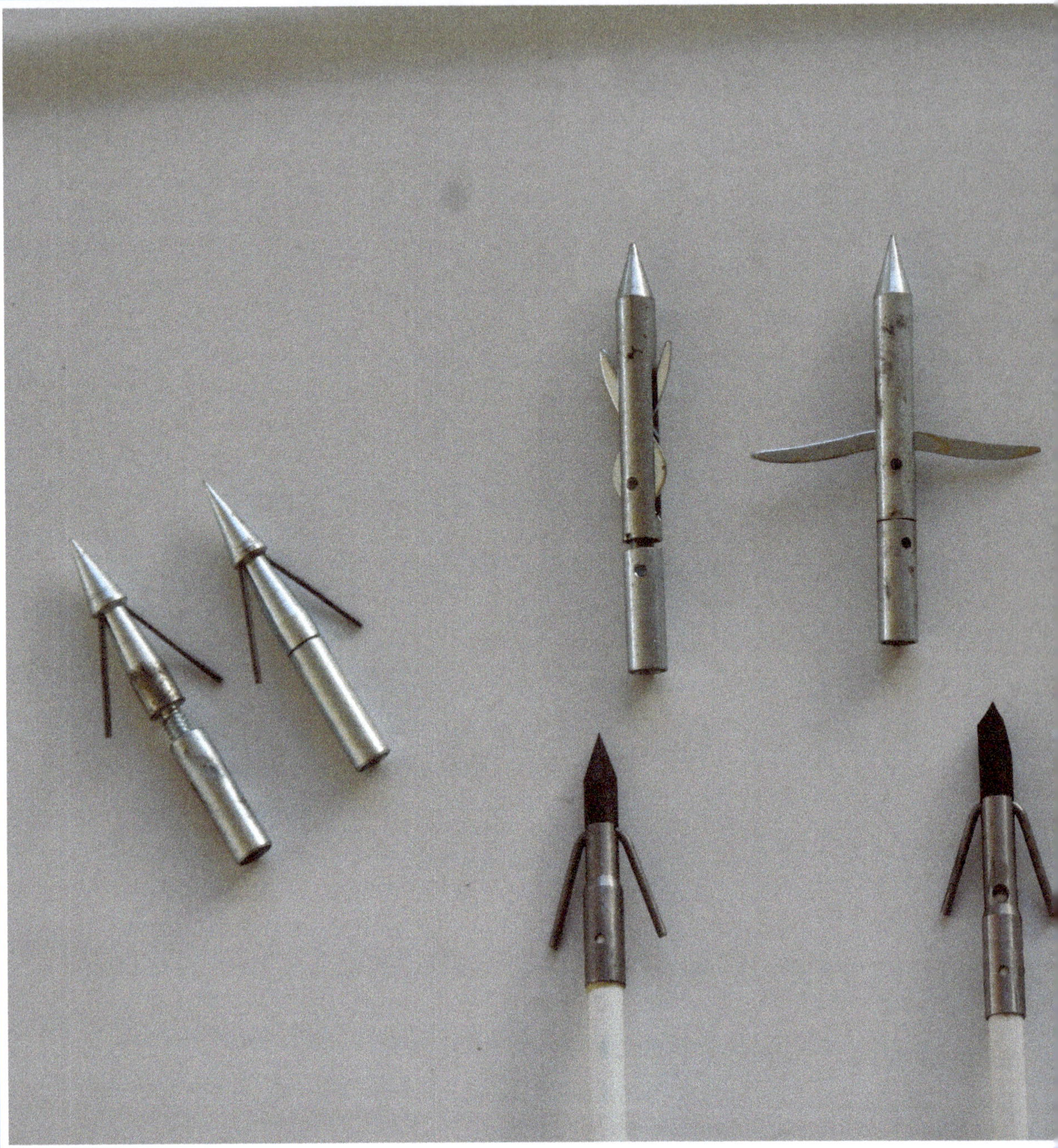

These bowfishing arrowheads are distinguished from regular arrowheads by the blades that fan out from their tips. These are designed to hook firmly into fish and prevent the arrow from slipping out of the swimming and thrashing target.

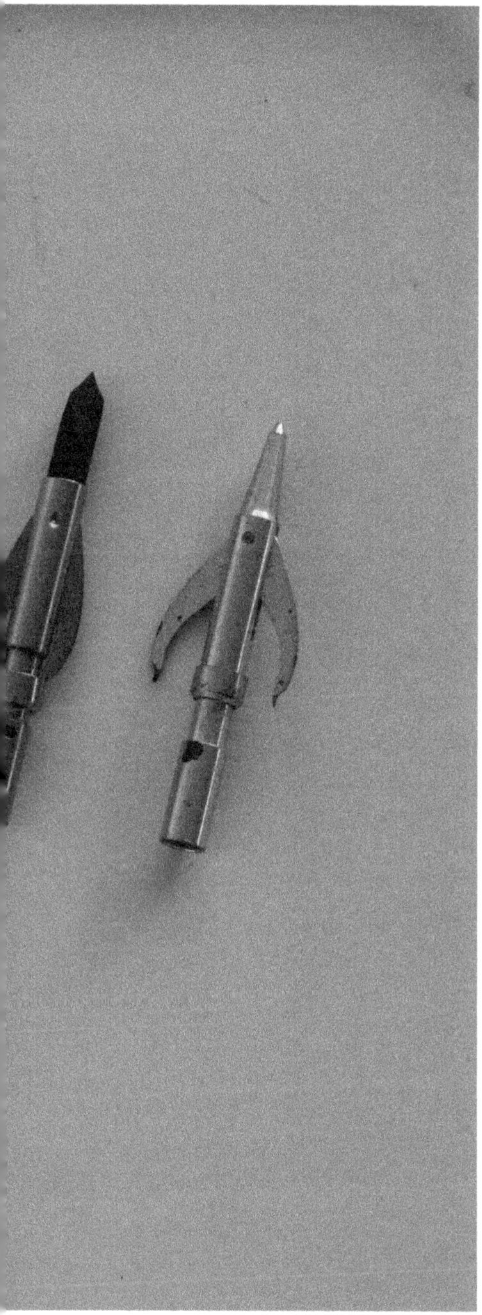

a little more costly and start at about $70. Some people like using these reels because they were specifically designed for bowfishing. Others stick with the less expensive reels.

Most hunting arrows are made out of lightweight materials, such as aluminum, and have hollow shafts. These arrows are usually too light to keep on course while traveling through water. Arrows made for bowfishing are typically heavier and stronger than arrows used for other types of archery. Most are made of fiberglass, though arrows made of solid aluminum and carbon fiber are also used.

Bowfishing arrows do not have fletching, which are the fins or vanes placed at the end of a conventional arrow to stabilize it while in flight toward its target. Fletching can cause an arrow to veer to one side underwater. Some bowfishers instead fit their arrows with lighted "nocks," which are the notched ends where the bowstring fits into the arrow. Lighted nocks makes it easier to find an arrow when bowfishing at night.

Bowfishing arrows also have special arrowheads. Most hunting arrowheads have sharp blades that fan out from the tip. Bowfishing arrows, however, have sharp tips and wire barbs designed to hook into the fish and hold the arrow in place.

Fishing line attaches to bowfishing arrows through a hole in the shaft or by using a safety slide. This is a device that mounts on the shaft of the arrow and is designed to prevent the line from snagging and the arrow from snapping back. Fishing line used by bowfishers usually has a test weight ranging from 80 to 200 pounds (36 to 91 kilograms). Be sure to use line that will be strong enough to haul in targeted fish without snapping.

Gearing Up

Bowfishers may want to pick up other accessories designed to make the sport easier. Both archery gloves and finger savers—which are tubes of soft, flexible material that wrap around bowstrings—are designed to protect fingers from the wear and tear of continually firing the bow. Some bowfishers use floats that attach to the line to help them locate the fish they shoot. Bowfishers sometimes bring fish out of the water with the aid of nets and gaffs. These are long sticks with sharp hooks attached at one end that are made for snaring fish and pulling them onto boats.

People who bowfish from boats also need to take along boating equipment. Life jackets and emergency floats are an absolute necessity for bowfishers. Boats should also be equipped with flashlights (and extra batteries), a first aid kit, and a fire extinguisher. An anchor and set of paddles should also be kept on board.

People who bowfish at night usually use lights powered by portable generators to help them see fish. Bowfishers who use generators should be aware of the dangers of using electricity on the water. Check generators, power cords, lights, and other electrical equipment for any damage or signs of wear before taking them out on the water.

Insect repellent can help keep mosquitoes and other pests at bay and should be worn day and night. Bowfishers who go out during the day should take along sunscreen and sunglasses to protect their eyes

Safety glasses, life vests, and head lanterns are just a few of the accessories that can make bowfishing both more safe and more successful.

and skin. Healthy snacks (like fruit, nuts, and granola bars) and non-caffeinated, nonalcoholic, and nonsugary drinks can help bowfishers keep their energy up during long outings. Be sure to take along fresh water to drink, especially when the sun is out.

CHAPTER 3

Bowfishing Basics

Bowfishing can be enjoyed under many varied conditions. Bowfishers often hit the water as soon as the season opens, usually in late spring. Many keep fishing until it closes, usually in late fall. They endure many kinds of weather and water conditions for their sport, from frigid northern rivers to southern swamps where alligators are common. Some bowfishers do all of their fishing close to home. Others may travel hundreds of miles to participate in tournaments or destination fishing.

Boating and "Walking the Shore"

Many bowfishers fish from boats. This is because it is easier to see fish in the water from a boat than it is to spot them from the shore or in the water. Flat-bottomed boats work best for bowfishing because it is easier to keep them stable when taking aim. Boats

A flat-bottomed boat is far more stable in the water than one with a rounded or V-shaped hull. The greater stability allows the boater to stand when aiming and firing arrows.

with engines are common. Be sure to follow any local guidelines for putting a boat in water, such as limits on how loud motors can be and whether lights can be used at night.

Bowfishing boats often have built-in platforms where bowfishers can stand. Bowfishers who fish at night may have their boats rigged with lights, especially halogen or metal halide lights. These bowfishers use portable gasoline-powered generators to power their lights. Bowfishers who use generators must be careful to keep their generators, lights, and power cords in good shape in order to avoid getting shocked or even electrocuted.

Boats are not essential to bowfishing, however. Many bowfishers fish either by wading in to the water or roaming along the bank, which is called "walking the shore." Many beginning bowfishers start out by walking the shore and eventually work up to using boats as they grow more skilled in and passionate about the sport. Bowfishers who want to fish from shore on privately owned land should make sure that they seek and receive permission to do so from the landowner.

Rivers and creeks are the most common sites for bowfishing, though some bowfishers go out on lakes, ponds, and even saltwater bays and estuaries. Clear, shallow water between 3 to 4 feet (0.9 to 1.2 m) deep is preferred because is easier to see fish and aim accurately in such shallow depths, and many of the fish species that are pursued by bowfishers tend to be found in shallow water.

Another reason that shallow water is preferred is that arrows slow down as they travel through water. The less water that an arrow must travel through, the greater its impact when it hits the fish. Remember, though, that even shallow water can be dangerous. Bowfishers should be aware of any water hazards that exist in the areas where they are fishing.

Day or Night?

A lot of bowfishers like to go fishing at night. As already mentioned, those that do so may rig up spotlights powered by batteries or generators to help them see fish. Night bowfishers find that shining

Bowfishing at night is a unique and thrilling experience. Be sure, however, to observe strict safety measures when operating generators and observe all local laws regarding the use of lights and generators at night.

a light into the water at night makes it easier to see the fish and aim accurately than is the case in daylight conditions.

People who like to bowfish during the day often go earlier in the season, near the time when fish are spawning in the spring. During spawning season, fish are very active and are seeking mates. In order to preserve and protect future fish populations, some states do not allow bowfishing during spawning season. Bowfishers should check for any such restrictions before planning an outing.

Bowfishers who like to go fishing at night may have the most success if they go during spawning time or in the fall when the water is usually clearest. Bowfishers who like to catch big fish should go in the summer months, when large fish are most active.

The Unique Challenges of Bowfishing

There are some specific challenges that bowfishers face that other fishers and archers never encounter. Aiming at a fish and hitting it with an arrow are very difficult skills, and they require a lot of practice. Light bends at the water's surface, which distorts how underwater objects look and where they appear to be from above water. A bowfisher who aims straight at a fish is likely to miss it because of this light distortion. The fish is actually deeper underwater and in a slightly different location than it appears to be from your perspective above the water's surface.

Bowfishers compensate for light distortion by aiming lower than where the fish appears to be. Laser sights can also help compensate for light distortion because laser light does not bend underwater. Some bowfishers practice aiming at targets placed underwater until they get a good feel for how to compensate for light distortion and aim accurately. Others simply spend a lot of time using their bows under a variety of conditions and learn by trial and error.

Nuisance or Delicacy?

A fish that is considered a rough fish by one culture may be a desirable game fish to another. For example, carp are commonly considered rough fish in the United States. However, carp are considered a desirable game fish in Europe and a valued food source in many parts of Asia.

Regional differences and preferences can also influence whether a fish is considered a rough fish or a desirable species. The long-nosed gar is considered a nuisance species in Ohio, for example. Yet in Louisiana, the same species is seen as a desirable food source by several ethnic groups.

One aiming technique that bowfishers use is called the "10-4 Rule." If the fish is 10 feet (3 m) away and 1 foot (30 centimeters) below the surface, the bowfisher should aim 4 inches (10 cm) low. Alter the calculation for fish that are farther away or deeper underwater. Bowfishers who double the distance or depth should also double the aiming point. For example, if the fish is 20 feet (6 m) away and 1 inch (2.5 cm) deep, aim 8 inches (20 cm) low. Other bowfishers use different systems. Some aim 6 inches (15 cm) low for every foot of depth. Others don't try to calculate the depth and simply aim 10 inches (25 cm) low.

Commonly Caught Fish

Most states allow bowfishers to catch only a few species of fish, referred to as "rough fish." The fish that bowfishers can catch are typically those that are undesirable to other fishers or are considered "nuisance"

These bowfishers have speared an alligator gar, a primitive ray-finned fish. Unlike other gars, the alligator gar possesses a dual row of large teeth in the upper jaw. These are what give it its name, along with its elongated snout. They can be as long as 10 feet (3 m) and weigh over 200 pounds (91 kg).

species. In some cases, these rough fish are invasive species that states are trying to eliminate from their waters. Invasive species typically compete for and consume resources shared with native species, and the native species can become stressed and die out. However, even some rough fish are listed as endangered and are protected by federal law.

There are many different species of rough fish that are legal to catch, depending on the state. They may be found in many different areas and vary a great deal in their habitat and behavior.

All species of carp found in the United States are considered invasive species. The common carp can tolerate many different conditions and a wide range of temperatures. They prefer large bodies of slow-moving or standing water with soft sediments or vegetation. They feed mostly on plant matter and can be found throughout the United States.

Silver carp and bighead carp are both filter feeders, meaning that they feed by straining water through their mouths and ingesting particles. Grass carp eat plant matter. They were originally brought to the United States from Asia to control aquatic weeds. They are commonly found in lakes, ponds, and still backwaters of large rivers. They can tolerate a wide range of temperatures and climates.

Unlike carp, gar are native to the United States. There are seven species of gar, and they can be found in freshwater and brackish water, as well as coastal swamps, in the eastern United States. Gar are noted for

Bowfishing from a rocky platform above the water can give you a better vantage point from which to locate fish and achieve better aim. It may also allow you to avoid being spotted by the fish.

their long, spear-like shape, armored scales, and elongated jaws filled with sharp teeth. Alligator gar are the most commonly fished gar species.

Other freshwater fish that are often targeted and caught by bowfishers include bowfin, suckers, some species of perch, and even catfish. Bowfishing for sharks and rays is often permitted in coastal areas. Some states even allow bowfishers to catch alligators and some species of turtles.

Bowfishing Strategies

Bowfishing requires skill, practice, and solid fishing strategies. Fish can detect shadows and motion on the water's surface. When bowfishing during the day, it may help to stalk fish from the cover of trees growing on the bank and to avoid making any sudden moves.

People who bowfish while wading may want to take advantage of any rocks that stick out above the water's surface. Standing above the water in this way can provide a vantage point that allows the bowfisher to get a better look at fish and aim more precisely. Try to stay in shaded areas in order to avoid being seen by fish.

Bowfishers who prefer to fish at night often use lights that shine down into the water to help mask the presence of their boats. The lights also help the bowfisher see fish and take aim. Remember to make sure that it is all right to use lights on the waterway before going out to bowfish. Some communities may not allow lights on the water after certain hours or at all.

Rough fish can sometimes be lured closer to the surface. The use of lights can sometimes achieve this. To tempt the fish to the surface, some bowfishers also use food as bait by strewing it across the water and letting it sink down. Common bait foods include breadcrumbs, corn, and specially formulated fish food, which can be bought in many sporting goods stores.

Two or more people bowfishing together can set up a "tag team" system. If one bowfisher misses a shot at a fish, his or her bowfishing partner can have a second arrow aimed at the fish and ready to be shot. Bowfishers working in such a way can increase the success of their fishing outing. Patience is needed after taking a shot at a fish. Fish can be skittish when their environment has been disturbed, and it may take some time for them to return to the site after an arrow has disturbed the waters.

CHAPTER 4

Handling Your Catch

At the end of a successful bowfishing outing, a bowfisher will have some impressive and tasty fish to take home. Bowfishers have many options regarding what to do with their catch. Some eat the fish. Others may be less enthusiastic about the idea of eating a rough fish, so they find another use for their catch. One common option for disposing of unwanted rough fish is to sell them or give them to farmers and gardeners who use the fish as fertilizer for their crops and gardens. Still others, particularly those who catch prize specimens, may want to have their catch mounted for display.

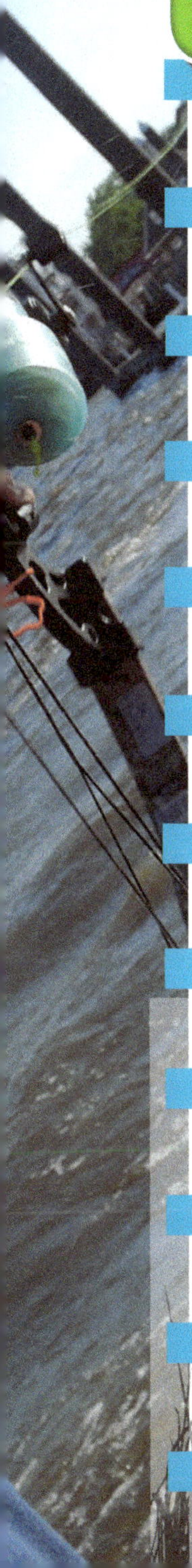

Keeping Fish Fresh

Fish that are caught by bowfishing are almost always killed in the process. Those that are not killed are usually so seriously injured that their chance of survival is very low. Catching and releasing fish is not an option for bowfishers

All fish that are caught and kept for later consumption should be put on ice immediately and stored cold until you are ready to clean and cook them.

because of the grievous bodily harm caused by the arrow. These fish should be killed as quickly and cleanly as possible in order to minimize their suffering.

Bowfishers who want to eat their catch will need to find a way to keep their fish fresh until they get home. Once home, they can cook their fish immediately or put the catch in the refrigerator or freezer for later. Fish spoil easily, and they should be kept cool and be cleaned soon after they are caught. Fish can be stored on ice in coolers. High catch limits make it easy for bowfishers to catch far more fish than they can store, and many bowfishers who do not intend to eat or mount their fish for display do not bother with keeping them fresh.

Cleaning the Fish

It is best to return to shore before cleaning fish. Cleaning a fish can be very messy. The process creates a lot of waste in the form of innards and discarded parts that most fishers do not want fouling their boats. Dumping such waste back into the water is considered unsporting by many fishers. It may even be illegal in some areas.

Cleaning a fish takes some practice. To start, make a shallow incision in the fish's belly running from just before the tail up to the head. Try not to cut too deeply to avoid puncturing the intestines. Gently spread the fish apart and scoop out the innards, using either your fingers or

Extreme care must be taken when cleaning a fish. The knives are sharp and the fish are slippery, which makes for a dangerous combination. Grippy, no-slip gloves help reduce the risk of accidental cuts.

a spoon. Wearing rubber gloves can help keep hands clean during this process. After the innards have been scooped out, cut off the head below the gills and remove the fins.

After removing the innards and head, remove the fish's scales (though a lot of fishermen skin or scale their catch before gutting or beheading it). This can be done by using a fish scaler or a large spoon to rake the fish's scales from the tail up to the head. This will cause the scales to flake off. After the scales have been removed, the fish is ready either to be cooked or frozen for later. Be sure to dispose of the waste parts properly. Fish heads, innards, and other waste parts can be disposed of in the garbage. In areas where composting is allowed, fish parts can be put in a compost pile and eventually used as a natural fertilizer.

Preparing Fish for Display

Fish that are going to be mounted for display should be handled with care. They should be kept cool immediately after being caught. It is recommended that they be wrapped in a damp towel and sealed in an airtight bag. Lay the fish on a piece of cardboard, and place another piece of cardboard on top of the fish to keep it flat. Carefully wrap tape around the cardboard to hold it in place, and keep the fish in a freezer until it can be taken to a taxidermist.

Before taking the fish to be mounted, think about how you want it to look. Mounted fish may be positioned so that they are stretched to their full length. They can also be mounted to look like they are turning or even leaping out of the water. Consider what kind of wood the fish will be mounted on and whether any details about how or when it was caught will be included on a label or plaque attached to the display.

People who mount fish and other wildlife are called taxidermists. There are taxidermists working in every state. Taxidermists vary in skill.

Why Are They Called Rough Fish?

The phrase "rough fish" originated in the Mississippi River valley in the mid-nineteenth century. At that time, commercial fishers in the United States would use nets to catch large numbers of fish. During the summer, they would have to get their fish to market as quickly as possible so that they could be sold before the entire catch spoiled. The fishers would keep the fully dressed fish—the ones that had been gutted and cut into fillets—that could be sold at full market value. They would discard fish that had been "dressed in the rough." This means that they had been gutted but not filleted, and therefore would not command a full price. These "rough fish" were tossed over the side of the boat, regardless of what species they were. The term eventually evolved to refer to any fish considered undesirable.

Some are capable of creating lifelike poses, while others do shoddy work. Ask other fishers or hunters who have well-mounted trophies on display to recommend a good taxidermist. You can also contact taxidermists listed in the phone book or online. Reputable taxidermists will be willing to show samples of their work and provide references and testimonials from other customers.

To Eat or Not to Eat?

Some bowfishers do not consider the rough fish that they catch to be edible. Others fish precisely because their sole purpose is to eat what

There's something about eating a fish, like this carp, that you have caught, cleaned, and cooked yourself that makes it taste extra delicious. Look online for great recipe ideas for the kind of fish you caught.

they catch. Arguments can be made for either position. Some rough fish are bottom feeders, meaning that they eat material found on the bottom of bodies of water. This can include decaying plant or animal matter. Some people do not like the idea of consuming fish that ingest such things. Other rough fish, such as carp, are very bony and are often perceived as more trouble to clean than they are worth.

All fish that are caught in the wild are exposed to chemicals and heavy metal pollutants, such as mercury. These toxins build up in fish, and predator fish that eat other fish often accumulate more mercury than other species. Most fish classified as rough fish carry low to moderate amounts of these toxins and are considered safe to eat in moderation.

In many parts of the world, rough fish are considered a valuable food source. This is particularly true of members of the carp family, which are eaten in many parts of Europe and Asia. There are many recipes available for these fish. Common preparations include fish stews and chowders, as well as baked and batter-dipped fish.

CHAPTER 5

BOWFISHING AND THE ENVIRONMENT

The bowfishing of rough fish species is often seen as having a positive impact on populations of more desirable fish. Eliminating invasive species of carp and other undesirable fish leaves more food for sport fish, such as trout or bass. It also helps rid waters of fish species that prey on other fish, particularly native and endangered species. However, bowfishing can also have a negative impact on the environment.

Critics of bowfishing point out that catch-and-release fishing, in which fish that are caught are quickly and carefully returned to the water, is not possible with bowfishing because the fish are almost always killed or too severely injured to survive. Critics also highlight the fact that some bowfishers simply throw away the fish that they catch, rather than eating them, using them for compost and fertilizer, or giving them away to someone who will eat or otherwise utilize the fish. Bowfishers are

It's important to be a responsible bowfisher. Be sure to use every fish you catch. Eat it, compost it, or give it to someone who will eat it or compost it. But never be careless and wasteful by simply throwing away a caught fish.

also frequently criticized for using lights at night and for the noise caused by their boats.

Bowfishers can help improve the image of the sport by following all local, state, and federal laws and regulations and behaving responsibly at all times. By becoming aware of environmental issues within the sport, its practitioners can work to minimize any negative impacts while also preserving the environment and fish populations for future generations of rod-and-reel fishers and bowfishers.

Overfishing

Overfishing is a global issue. As the number of people on the planet continues to grow rapidly, stress on the food chain increases. This is true of fish found in saltwater and in freshwater environments.

The fish that bowfishers catch usually are not threatened by overfishing. Most states allow bowfishers to catch only fish that are considered invasive or nuisance species. Even so, limits are usually in place for the number of nuisance fish that can be caught. These limits allow the fish population to remain in check without dying off completely. Sometimes, these fish include native species, such as varieties of catfish or gar that may be becoming scarce in some areas. States often put limits on how many of these fish can be caught, but some unethical bowfishers may ignore these limits.

Some bowfishers catch protected species, either accidentally or intentionally. Some protected species resemble fish that can be caught, and it is sometimes hard to be sure of a fish's species from above water. When in doubt, do not shoot an arrow. Be absolutely sure that you are targeting a rough fish before loosing your arrow. Bowfishing in protected waters can harm fish populations. Bowfishers who are caught exceeding their catch limits, catching protected species, or fishing in protected areas can face hefty fines.

Be sure to respect all catch limits when bowfishing. Even rough fish may have catch limits, so check all local regulations before heading out.

Pollution

Pollution is not a problem that is unique to bowfishing. Careless fishers of all types are guilty of polluting waters and shores. Pollution does not just extend to tossing empty containers and food wrappers into the water. For example, fuel from poorly maintained boats can seep into the water, poisoning fish and other wildlife.

Lost arrows and broken lines that are left in the water can also harm wildlife. Fish, birds, and animals may be cut by discarded arrows. Wildlife can become tangled in old fishing line, which limits their ability to move and escape from predators. Old fishing line can also kill wildlife by strangling animals or choking off the flow of blood to their limbs.

The Bowfishing Association of America

The Bowfishing Association of America (BAA) was founded in 1990 in Little Rock, Arkansas, with the purpose of promoting the sport of bowfishing throughout the United States. One of the group's main missions is to support those environmental programs that help keep habitats and waterways clean and healthy.

The BAA encourages its members to take care of their favorite bowfishing sites and to obey all local, state, and federal laws and regulations. The group provides information about bowfishing techniques and concerns and links together a wide network of state and local bowfishing groups. In addition to providing help and information to its members, the BAA hosts the annual Bowfishing World Championship and provides insurance and support to state and local tournaments throughout the nation.

Guides and Tourism

Some bowfishers work as guides for those who are beginners to the sport. For a fee, they take new bowfishers out on the water and show them the basics. A trip out with a guide can be a perfect introduction to bowfishing for people who don't know other bowfishers whom they can go out with and from whom they can learn more about the sport.

Prospective bowfishers should be careful when choosing a guide. Be sure to pick a guide who has a good reputation for safety and respecting the law and the environment.

Guides who ignore the law, bowfish in restricted areas, and behave in an unsportsmanlike manner should be avoided. These guides may set a bad example for new bowfishers to follow and teach them bad habits and practices. Responsible guides can be found by looking online or asking around at sporting goods stores. Ask a prospective guide for references from other bowfishers to make sure that he or she is knowledgeable, safe, and responsible.

States set guidelines for where bowfishing is allowed. Some of these sites may see heavy use, particularly those areas where tournaments are held. Having a large number of bowfishers gather in one place, even if they are respectful and responsible, can have a negative impact on other species. Birds and animals may avoid these places for some time afterward, and native plants may be damaged. Respect areas that are off-limits to bowfishing. These areas may be ecologically fragile.

Benefiting the Environment

Many bowfishers understand that in order for their sport to continue, they need to protect the places where they fish. They recognize that by taking only fish that are considered nuisance or invasive species, they are benefiting other species. While bowfishers enjoy the thrill of catching fish, they also enjoy being out on the water and in nature. By protecting the environment, they can be sure of having ecologically healthy places to bowfish and thriving fish populations to target for years to come.

Bowfishers may take direct action to benefit the environment. Many bowfishers take part in waterway cleanups by helping pick up litter. Some bowfishers also help scientists by keeping tallies of the fish and aquatic wildlife that they see. This can help scientists keep track of changes in the environment.

Introducing others to bowfishing is a good way to help increase awareness of threats to waterways. Teaching new bowfishers to appreciate and respect nature will help them enjoy the sport and prepare them for the day when they, in turn, might teach others how to bowfish.

Glossary

aquatic Living or growing in water.

compound bow A bow whose holding weight when at full draw is less than the peak weight at which the arrow is projected.

ecological Relating to the environment and the way in which plants, animals, and humans live together and interact with each other.

excursion A short trip taken for pleasure.

fletching The feathers attached to the rear of an arrow that stabilize it during flight.

format The organization, plan, style, layout, or type of something.

gaff An iron hook with a handle used for landing large fish.

generator A device for converting one form of energy into another.

habitat The natural environment of an organism.

invasive species Organisms not native to a region that, when introduced, cause economic or environmental harm or harm to animal and human health.

longbow A weapon for shooting arrows made from a long, curved piece of wood or other flexible material and a string.

mercury A heavy, silver-white, highly toxic metallic element.

nock A metal or plastic piece at the end of an arrow, having a notch for the bowstring. Also, the act of adjusting an arrow to a bowstring in preparation for shooting.

novice A person who is new to or inexperienced in a certain task, activity, or situation.

nuisance An obnoxious or annoying person, thing, condition, or practice.

reel A cylinder, frame, or other device that turns on an axis and is used to wind up or pay out something, such as fishing line.

rough fish Any fish that is not valued as a sport fish or considered a significant source of food by sport fishers.

shaft An elongated cylinder-shaped pole forming the body of various weapons, such as arrows or spears.

sight Device used to direct one's aim at a target.

swivel A fastening device that allows the thing fastened to turn around freely upon it, especially to turn in a full circle.

taxidermy The art of preparing and preserving the skins of animals and of stuffing and mounting them in lifelike form.

vendor A person or agency that sells a product or service.

For More Information

Archery Hall of Fame
58 North Main Street
Union City, PA 16438
(814) 392-8901
Web site: http://www.archeryhalloffame.com
The hall of fame recognizes excellence in the sport of archery.

***Bowfisher* Magazine**
HC 79, Box 3240
Pittsburg, MO 65724
Web site: http://www.thebowfisher.com
Bowfisher is the only magazine dedicated to bowfishing.

Bowfishing Association of America
5 Eldon Starr Lane
Conway, AR 72032
Web site: http://www.bowfishingassociation.com
The Bowfishing Association of America advocates for bowfishers and for the sport of bowfishing.

Canadian Parks and Wilderness Society
506–250 City Centre Avenue
Ottawa, ON K1R 6K7
Canada
(800) 333-9453
Web site: http://www.cpaws.org
This organization focuses on protecting many important areas of Canada's wilderness.

Environment Canada
Inquiry Centre
10 Wellington, 23rd Floor
Gatineau, QC K1A 0H3
Canada
(819) 997-2800
Web site: http://www.ec.gc.ca
Environment Canada is the government agency charged with environmental protection and conservation.

Field & Stream
2 Park Avenue
New York, NY 10016
(212) 779-5012
Web site: http://www.fieldandstream.com
Field & Stream magazine is devoted to the outdoor experience and lifestyle.

National Field Archery Association
800 Archery Lane
Yankton, SD 57078
(605) 260-9279
Web site: http://www.nfaa-archery.org
The National Field Archery Association is dedicated to the sport of archery and the conservation and preservation of game and its natural habitat.

U.S. Fish and Wildlife Service
1849 C Street NW

Washington, DC 20240
(800) 344-9453
Web site: http://www.fws.gov
The U.S. Fish and Wildlife Service is dedicated to the conservation, protection, and enhancement of wildlife, plants, and their habitats.

Web Sites

Due to the changing nature of Internet links, Rosen Publishing has developed an online list of Web sites related to the subject of this book. This site is updated regularly. Please use this link to access the list:

http://www.rosenlinks.com/FISH/Bow

For Further Reading

Beatty, Richard. *Wetlands*. Chicago, IL: Raintree, 2011.

Bourne, Wade. *Basic Fishing: A Beginner's Guide*. New York, NY: Skyhorse Publishing, 2011.

Buffler, Ron, and Tom Dickson. *Fishing for Buffalo: A Guide to the Pursuit and Cuisine of Carp, Suckers, Eelpout, Gar, and Other Rough Fish*. Minneapolis, MN: University of Minnesota Press, 2009.

Drake, Jane, and Ann Love. *Alien Invaders: Species That Threaten Our World*. Plattsburg, NY: Tundra Books, 2009.

Gross, W.H. *Young Beginner's Guide to Shooting and Archery: Tips for Gun and Bow*. Minneapolis, MN: Creative Publishing International, 2009.

Herrigal, Eugen. *Zen in the Art of Archery*. New York, NY: Vintage Books/Random House, 1999.

Kasabian, David, and Anna Kasabian. *Wild Fish Cookbook: Recipes from North America's Top Fishing Lodges*. Minneapolis, MN: Creative Publishing International, 2007.

Klein, Adam G. *Archery* (Outdoor Adventure!). Edina, MN: Checkerboard Books, 2008.

Kurlansky, Mark. *World Without Fish: How Could We Let This Happen?* New York, NY: Workman Publishing, 2011.

McMahon, Tyler, and Paul Diamond. *Fishing's Greatest Misadventures*. San Diego, CA: Casagrande Press, 2008.

Meitin, Patrick. *The Bowhunter's Guide to Better Shooting*. Palm Coast, FL: Petersen's Bowhunting, 2011.

Nickens, T. Edward, ed. *The Total Outdoorsman Manual* (Field & Stream). New York, NY: Weldon Owen, 2011.

Page, Lawrence M., and Brooks M. Burr. *Peterson Field Guide to Freshwater Fishes*. Second Edition. Boston, MA: Houghton Mifflin Harcourt, 2011.

Pope, Saxton. *Hunting with the Bow and Arrow*. Charleston, SC: BiblioLife, 2008.

Rafferty, John P. *Rivers and Streams* (Living Earth). New York, NY: Rosen Publishing, 2011.

Robb, Bob. *The Field & Stream Bowhunting Handbook*. Guilford, CT: Lyons Press, 2007.

Smith, William Hovey. *Archer's Bible Presents: Practical Bowfishing*. Accokeek, MD: Stoeger Publishing Company, 2005.

Adams, Chuck. *Bowhunter's Digest*. Northbrook, IL: DBI Books, 1990.

Anderson, Dennis. "Bright Lights, Big Carp." *Minneapolis Star-Tribune*, June 10, 2012. Retrieved August 2012 (http://www.startribune.com/sports/outdoors/158315735.html?refer=y).

Appleberg, Christine. "Bowfishing Tournaments: More Popular Than Ever!" HuntingNet.com, July 21, 2006. Retrieved September 2012 (http://www.huntingnet.com/fieldjournal/fieldjournal_detail.aspx?nID=419).

Baron, Frank. *What Fish Don't Want You to Know: An Insider's Guide to Freshwater Fishing*. Camden, ME: Ragged Mountain Press, 2003.

Bostian, Kelly. "Economical, Ecological Bowfishing Grows in Popularity with Kids." *Tulsa World*, July 3, 2011. Retrieved August 2012 (http://www.tulsaworld.com/sportsextra/article.aspx?subjectid=29&articleid=20110703_29_B7_CUTLIN844631).

Bowman, Dale. "Bowfishing the Illinois a Slaughter on the Water." *Chicago Sun-Times*, September 21, 2005. Retrieved August 2012 (http://www.highbeam.com/doc/1P2-1591677.html).

Cocking, Susan. "Bowfishing at Night Presents Unique Challenges." *Miami Herald*, July 5, 2012. Retrieved August 2012 (http://www.miamiherald.com/2012/07/05/2882069/bowfishing-at-night-presents-unique.html).

Crable, Ad. "Part Hunting, Part Fishing—Meet Bowfishing." Lancaster Online, June 15, 2010. Retrieved September 2012 (http://lancasteronline.com/article/local/259865_OUTDOORS--Part-hunting--part-fishing---meet-bowfishing.html).

Daily Mail. "Monster Meets Its Match: Record-Breaking Alligator Gar Fish Caught in Mississippi Lake." February 21, 2011. Retrieved August 2012 (http://www.dailymail.co.uk/news/article-1358616/Record-breaking-alligator-caught-Mississippi-lake.html).

Kaminsky, Peter, and Greg Schwipps. *Fishing for Dummies*. Indianapolis, IN: Wiley Publishing, 2011.

Lynch, Jim. "Archer Draws Aim on Carp." *Detroit News*, December 4, 2009. Retrieved August 2012 (http://www.glu.org/fr/asiancarp/headlines/archer-draws-aim-carp).

Maas, David R. *The Complete Guide to Freshwater Fishing*. Minnetonka, MN: Creative Publishing International, 2002.

Marlow, Roy S. *Timeless Bowhunting*. Mechanicsburg, PA: Stackpole Books, 2003.

McCoy, John. "Bowhunting on the Internet." *Sunday Gazette-Mail*, August 12, 2012. Retrieved August 2012 (http://www.wvgazette.com/Outdoors/201208110044).

Meersman, Tom. "Cities May Soon Add Bowfishing to Their Quiver." *Minneapolis Star-Tribune*, September 17, 2012. Retrieved September 2012 (http://www.startribune.com/local/169978806.html?page=all&prepage=7&c=y&refer=y).

Murrell, Marc. "Dry Summer Aids Bowfishermen." *Topeka Capital Journal*, August 26, 2012. Retrieved September 2012 (http://cjonline.com/sports/2012-08-25/outdoors-dry-summer-aids-bowfishermen).

Powell, Allen. "Gretna Fishing Guide Indicted in Federal Court on Wednesday." *Times-Picayune*, September 21, 2011. Retrieved August 2012 (http://www.nola.com/crime/index.ssf/2011/09/gretna_fishing_guide_indicted.html).

Sorrells, Brian J. *Beginner's Guide to Traditional Archery*. Mechanicsburg, PA: Stackpole Books, 2004.

Toth, Mike. *The Complete Idiot's Guide to Fishing Basics*. Indianapolis, IN: Alpha Books, 2000.

Weisberg, Deborah. "Arrows Point the Way to a New Angle on an Old Game." *Pittsburgh Post-Gazette*, June 23, 2002. Retrieved August

2012 (http://old.post-gazette.com/sports/outdoors/20020623 weisberg0623p3.asp).

Wesbrock, Jason R. "Learn the Bowfishing Basics." HuntingNet.com. Retrieved August 2012 (http://www.huntingnet.com/articles/article _detail.aspx?articles_id=504).

INDEX

About the Author

Jason Porterfield is a writer and journalist living in Chicago, Illinois. He has written more than twenty books for the Rosen Publishing Group, including several on basketball, baseball, and other sports-related topics. He grew up fishing in the Blue Ridge Mountains of Virginia.

About the Consultant

Benjamin Cowan has more than twenty years of both freshwater and saltwater angling experience. In addition to being an avid outdoorsman, Cowan is a member of many conservation organizations. He currently resides in west Tennessee.

Photo Credits

Cover, back cover, pp. 1, 3, 7, 12–13, 14, 18, 20, 28, 33, 39, 43, 46, 50 Mira Oberman/AFP/Getty Images; pp. 4–5, 7, 14, 18, 20, 28, 33, 39, 43, 46, 50 (water) © iStockphoto.com/MichaelJay; pp. 5, 16, 19, 21, 24–25, 29, 36–37, 49 Hovey Smith; pp. 8, 10, 27, 34–35, 47 Mark Lee/Bowfishing Association of America; pp. 30–31 Wichita Eagle/McClatchy-Tribune/Getty Images; p. 40 Jessie Eldora Robertson/Shutterstock.com; p. 41 Wong Hock weng/Shutterstock.com; pp.44–45 Vitaliy Hrabar/Shutterstock.com; back cover and interior silhouettes (figures) © iStockphoto.com/A-Digit, Hemera/Thinkstock; back cover and interior silhouette (grass) © iStockphoto.com/Makhnach_M; back cover silhouette (hook) iStockphoto.com/Jason Derry.

Designer: Nicole Russo; Photo Researcher: Marty Levick